Gordon and the New Girl

Three kids, one friendship, and a bunch of crazy adventures!

THIRD-GRADE Friends

Gordon and the New Girl

by Suzanne Williams

Illustrated by George Ulrich

A
LITTLE APPLE
PAPERBACK

SCHOLASTIC INC.

New York   Toronto   London   Auckland   Sydney
Mexico City   New Delhi   Hong Kong   Buenos Aires

ISBN 0-439-32991-4

12 11 10 9 8 7 6 5 4 3 2 1   3 4 5 6 7 8/0
40

Printed in the U.S.A.
First printing, March 2003

"One who finds a friend finds a treasure."
                                        – Italian proverb

To Leslie Engel, treasured friend through
            distance and time.

Contents

Gordon and the New Girl

1
"My Name Is Gordon"

Tuesday morning at school I sharpened all my pencils and lined them up in my pencil box beside my pens and markers. Then I straightened the folders and books inside my desk. I like being well prepared, so I do this every morning before school starts. My two best friends, Hilary and Josh, like to tease me about my neatness.

"I've heard of fussy eaters," Josh commented once. "But you, Gordon, are the only person I know who's a fussy *neater*."

I can't help it. It's just the way I am.

I set my spelling book on top of my desk. Spelling is our first subject on Tuesday mornings. The bell rang. Sitting up straight, I gave Ms. Foster, our third-grade teacher, my full attention. Most of the other kids were still talking to friends or looking for stuff in their desks.

Ms. Foster smiled at me. "Gordon is

ready to listen," she said. "How about the rest of you?"

I cringed. I'm glad my teacher likes me, but sometimes I wish she wouldn't say things like that. Hilary and Josh don't seem to mind, but I think it makes some of the other kids feel bad. I don't really like being a teacher's pet. And I don't understand why Ms. Foster needs one, anyway. She's got a *dog* at home!

The door opened, and Alicia, who sits two seats across from me in class, stepped into the room, followed by another girl. Alicia spoke quietly to Ms. Foster. So quietly, I couldn't hear what she was saying even though I sit in the front row.

In a minute Ms. Foster clapped her hands together. "Boys and girls," she said, "Alicia has brought a special guest with her today." She smiled at the girl who stood beside Alicia. The girl had long, shiny black hair and glasses.

"This is María," Ms. Foster said. "She's Alicia's cousin. María is here on vacation from Mexico and will be staying to work with us the rest of the week. I hope you'll make her feel welcome."

I knew that in Mexico people speak Spanish and I wondered if María knew English. She hadn't said anything so far, so maybe she didn't. Or maybe she only knew a little. María followed Alicia to the front row and sat down at the empty desk between Alicia and me.

"Hel-lo," I said, speaking slowly so María would understand me. Then I pointed to myself. "My name is Gordon," I said, pronouncing each word carefully. "Gordon," I repeated. I poked a finger at my chest.

María smiled. Butterfly-shaped clips glittered in her shiny black hair. She pointed at me. "Gor-don," she said slowly.

"That's right!" I told her. "Very good."

María laughed. Then peering at me through her glasses, she leaned toward me. "You don't have to speak to me like I'm a two-year-old," she whispered. "My English isn't *that* bad."

Warmth spread from my neck to my face. *Good grief.* How could I have made such a stupid mistake? "S-sorry," I stuttered. Hiding my face in my spelling book, I pretended to study the words. Why hadn't I kept my mouth shut? If only my mind worked as fast as my mouth.

2
Eggs-tinct

At morning recess, I escaped to the playground with Hilary and Josh. We hurried to be first in line at the wall-ball courts. Josh bounced a yellow rubber ball up and down. "I'm going to beat both of you this morning," he said, grinning. Then he wiggled his ears, which, as Hilary often teases him, stick out from his head like two big mushrooms.

Hilary and I laughed. "Dream on, Josh,"

7

Hilary said. She grabbed the ball away and tossed it up in the air.

Josh is not a bad wall-ball player, in fact, he's pretty good. But Hilary is the best in our class, and, most of the time, I'm second best.

We played rock, paper, scissors to decide who would serve first, and Hilary won. "Okay, Josh," Hilary said, bouncing the ball up and down a few times. "Now's your chance to make your dream come true."

Hilary struck the ball with one fist. It bounced on the ground, hit the brick wall of the school just above the service line, and dropped close to the wall. Josh raced to get the return. He smacked the ball. It thumped on the ground, then hit high on the wall.

Hilary was waiting. She slammed the ball so hard Josh was forced to run backward to get the next return. Then Hilary hit a soft one and Josh had to run up close again. Hilary made him run forward and backward several more times before finishing him off with a great shot that landed just inside the court.

"Phew," said Josh. "You sure know how to turn a perfectly good dream into a nightmare."

Hilary grinned. "There's always the *next* recess."

Seven or eight other kids were in line behind me as I stepped up to play Hilary. Most of them — Carl, Mark, Stephanie, and Nicola — were from my class. I looked around for Alicia and María but didn't see them. Good. I didn't want to embarrass myself in front of María again if Hilary beat me — which seemed likely after the way she'd just whipped Josh.

I crouched low, keeping an eye on Hilary and the ball. "Ready to be eggs-terminated?"

I asked. That's a chicken joke. I tell a lot of them. For reasons I'd rather not go into, my nickname with Hilary and Josh is "Chicken Boy." Let's just say I sometimes eggs-hibit chickenlike behavior. Especially when I'm worried or afraid.

Hilary laughed. "I'm going to make you eggs-tinct." Then she tossed the ball in the air and let it bounce on the ground once. "Double!" she shouted, slamming into the ball with both hands clasped together.

The ball slapped the ground, then bounced off the wall. I'd been watching the direction of Hilary's swing and calculated where the ball would land. But just as I was about to swing, someone cried out, "Come on, Gor-don! Smash it!"

María! Startled, I took my eyes off the ball for an instant and swung too late. The only thing my hands made contact with was *air*.

My face hot, I glanced around for María as I left the court, but she'd disappeared. She had to have seen my air ball before she left, though. *Good grief.*

"That was a quick eggs-it," Josh teased as I joined him at the back of the line.

I shrugged. As Hilary says, there's always the *next* recess. But I wished María hadn't been watching. She must think I'm a

11

real loser. Especially after the way I talked to her this morning.

When recess ended, Hilary, Josh, and I walked back to class together. "So what do you think of the new girl, Alicia's cousin?" I couldn't help asking.

"She seemed kind of quiet when Ms. Foster introduced her," said Hilary. "But wasn't that her yelling, just before you missed the ball?"

My face grew warm again. "Don't know," I lied. "Could've been."

"Was her name Marcia?" asked Josh. "Or Mary?"

"Neither," I said. "It's *María*." Her name sounded musical to me. Like it should be sung, instead of spoken. "*María*," I repeated, letting my voice rise and fall.

Josh and Hilary looked at each other

with raised eyebrows. "I think Gordon likes the new girl," said Hilary.

"Aww, man. Say it isn't true, Gordon," Josh said. "I couldn't stand it if you started going all mushy on us."

"Don't be ridiculous," I snorted. "I just think she's kind of interesting, that's all."

Hilary grinned. "*I* think it's interesting that *you* think she's interesting."

Josh frowned. "Interesting how?"

"I-I don't know," I said. "She's from Mexico, of course. That's interesting. And she speaks English perfectly." I paused. "I think she must be very smart. I'd like to observe her and find out more about her."

"*Observe* her?" Josh laughed. "Now I feel better. Sounds like what you'd say if you were looking at a bug. Like a rare beetle, maybe."

Hilary eyed me. "Or a *butterfly*?"

I gulped, wondering if she'd caught me staring at the silver clips in María's shiny black hair. Could Hilary be right about my liking María? I'd never noticed much about other girls before.

3
Lunch Trouble

When I sat down at my desk after recess I tried not to look at María. I was afraid to, in case Hilary was right. Making friends has never been easy for me, but I had no idea how to act around a girl who I liked. Besides, María wouldn't *want* me looking at her if she thought I was a loser.

Not looking wasn't easy, though. During math, without meaning to, I glanced up after finishing a story problem and saw that María wasn't working out of the same math book as the rest of the class. "Did you bring your own math book with you?" I couldn't help asking.

María looked up and smiled. "Yes."

"I love math," I said. "I can't wait till we do harder long division problems."

María adjusted her glasses. "I love long division, too. But dividing fractions is such a challenge."

My eyes almost popped out of my head when she said that. "You know how to divide fractions already?" I exclaimed.

María smiled again. "I'm not very good at it yet. We were just learning how to do it before I left on vacation."

I was impressed. I was sure multiplying and dividing fractions wasn't something I'd get to learn until next year or even the year after.

At lunchtime, Josh and Hilary brought their lunches to my desk so we could eat together like we usually do. Today's school lunch was spaghetti and green beans, and I was *starved*. After taking a long sip from my milk carton, I stabbed at a wad of spaghetti noodles that were all stuck together.

As I brought a huge forkful up to my mouth, I spotted Alicia sitting with Nicola and Stephanie at the back of the room. María stood in the middle of the room, lunch sack in hand. She glanced around the room, obviously looking for Alicia.

Hilary saw me watching. "Want me to ask her to eat with us?"

Thrusting my fork into my mouth, I blushed. *Did I want María to eat with us?*

The idea was exciting and terrifying at the same time.

Josh frowned. "Ask who to eat with us?"

Hilary didn't answer. Instead she waved at María.

María looked our way. She seemed to smile directly at me.

With horror, I realized that several long spaghetti noodles were dangling from my

mouth. *Good grief.* I slurped them up, and sauce splattered all over my chin. I grabbed for my napkin and knocked over my milk carton. It splashed across my desk and dripped onto the floor. "Oh, no!" I cried.

"Smooth move," said Josh, but he grabbed his own napkin and wiped the milk off the top of my desk while Hilary ran to get some paper towels for the floor.

"Sorry," I apologized after Hilary was back.

"No big deal," said Hilary as we scrubbed the floor clean with the paper towels.

"At least you're not as clumsy as I am," Josh said. "I even trip over the cords of cordless phones."

"Ha-ha," I said. I looked around for María, but by now she was eating with Alicia and her friends. Mostly I was relieved. For some reason, things seemed to go wrong whenever she was near.

4
Black Holes

After lunch recess on Tuesdays we have PE. Today Ms. Smith, the PE teacher, divided us into two teams to play dodgeball. Hilary, Josh, and I were all on the same team. María was on the opposite team with Alicia and some others. Ms. Smith gave each team five balls. Then she blew her whistle to start the game.

I was doing fine, running around and

dodging the other team's balls, when a ball rolled up to my feet. I scooped it up, then looked around for a target. María stood sideways to me, just a few feet across the centerline. I could tell she didn't see me. She had a ball in her hands, and, as I watched, she lobbed it at Mark but missed. I could've hit her easily, especially now that she didn't have a ball to throw at me, but for some reason, I just couldn't do it. It was like the ball was glued to my hands!

"What are you waiting for?" Josh yelled, coming up behind me. "Throw it at her!"

María wheeled around. For a second neither of us moved. We just stared at each other. Then María shrieked and darted away. Josh grabbed the ball out of my hands and threw it at her, but she was far enough away by then that he missed.

Josh rolled his eyes at me. "Are you nuts, or something? You could've gotten her out!"

"Sorry," I said.

At the end of the game, my team lost.

"Why didn't you throw the ball at me when you had the chance?" María whispered later when we were back in class doing silent reading.

I looked up from my book and blushed. "I don't know."

María stared at me through her glasses. "I would've thrown it at you," she said. Then she went back to reading her own book.

She would've? Well, of course she would've. That's how the game is *supposed* to be played. What was wrong with me, anyway? If it'd been any other girl, I wouldn't have had any trouble throwing that ball.

I glanced down at my book, which was about black holes. Normally I love reading about astronomy, but today my mind kept wandering from the words on the page. Several times I found myself staring at the glittery butterfly clips in María's shiny black hair.

Suddenly it occurred to me that María was like a black hole! Just as a black hole captures light, María had captured *me*. Light behaves oddly when it gets close to a black hole, and I was behaving oddly, too. I'm usually a very neat and tidy person, yet today I'd knocked over my milk and splattered spaghetti sauce all over my chin. At morning recess, I'd air-balled an easy wall-ball return, then froze when I should've thrown a ball at María during PE. I've always been a good worker, but today I had the concentration powers of a speck of dust.

As if to prove it, my mind wandered again, and I found myself wondering if María liked astronomy as much as I do. *I have a telescope at home*, I thought. *If she came over, we could look through my telescope together at the craters on the moon. The moon is supposed to be romantic and . . .* Good grief! What was wrong with me? I shuddered. Josh had hit the nail on the head. I *must* be going nuts. But at the same time, I really did want to get to know María better.

I leaned over, trying to see what she was

reading, but I couldn't make out the title of her book. If I lean just a little farther to the right I'd be able to see the cover. I stretched a few more inches. Suddenly my chair tipped, and I tumbled onto the floor, right at María's feet.

María's glasses slid to the end of her nose as she looked down at me. "Are you all right?" she asked, pushing her glasses back up.

My mouth opened and closed, but no words came out. It was like they'd been sucked away. I panicked. Who knew what might happen if I stayed near her a moment longer? Leaping to my feet, I rushed out the door and ran to the restroom.

5
Girl Trouble

I stayed in the restroom for a long time, worrying about what I would do to keep away from María for the rest of the afternoon. When I finally did return to class, María was standing at the front of the room answering questions from the class about Mexico. It was social studies time and we'd been studying other countries. Ms. Foster must've asked María to share.

I slid into my seat as Hilary asked María what city she lived in.

"Mexico City," María replied.

"That's the capital of Mexico, isn't it?" asked Nicola. "It's a *huge* city."

María nodded. "Over eight million people."

Someone whistled.

"Can you teach us some Spanish words?" asked Carl.

"Sure," said María. "But Alicia speaks Spanish, too. Tell us what you want to know."

Within minutes, María, with Alicia helping, had taught us the numbers from one (*uno*) to ten (*diez*) and how to say hello (*hola*), good-bye (*adiós*), and thank you (*gracias*).

"Could you teach us some swear words?" Mark asked.

Ms. Foster frowned. "That's not appropriate," she said.

"Here's one you can use that's okay," said María. "If you accidentally fall off your chair" — she glanced at me, and I blushed — "or get a 'zero' on a test, you can say '¡Caramba!'" She hit her forehead as she said it.

Everyone laughed.

María said *caramba* was kind of like saying *darn*.

We practiced the word over and over, till Ms. Foster made us stop. After that, Ms. Foster showed a long video about family life and customs in countries around the world. She always lets us sit wherever we want when we watch movies, so I grabbed my chair and carried it to the back of the room to sit beside Josh. I hoped that if I sat far away from María my behavior would return to normal.

Since the video was over an hour long, Ms. Foster said we would skip afternoon recess so we could finish the film before the end of the day.

"*Caramba*," Josh said. He hates missing recess.

But I was secretly glad. If María chose to hang around the wall-ball courts during recess, I wouldn't be able to play worth beans, anyway.

Ms. Foster ran a hand through her dark hair which was so wild today she looked like she'd been out in a windstorm. "I'll give you an extra recess later in the week," she said.

"I bet she'll forget," Josh grumbled in my ear.

"You can remind her if she does," I whispered back.

When the bell rang at the end of the day, relief flooded over me. I grabbed my jacket and backpack from the coat racks and slipped out the door with Hilary and Josh.

"What was up with you today?" Hilary asked as we began to walk.

My breath caught in my throat. "What do you mean?"

Hilary and Josh exchanged a look. "Other people spill their milk and fall off chairs, but not you, Gordon," Hilary said.

Josh frowned. "Hilary's right. You've been acting strange all day. We think it's because of the new girl, Martina."

"María," I corrected him.

Josh grinned. He knew María's name all

right. I guess he was trying to be funny. But I didn't like him joking about her name.

Josh kicked a rock as we crossed the school grounds. "Take my advice. Stay away from the new girl. Girls are trouble."

"Hmpf!" Hilary slugged Josh in the shoulder.

Josh rubbed his arm. "I didn't mean *you*."

I knew what Josh meant, of course. Hilary's not like other girls. But I didn't see how I could stay away from María when she sat right next to me in class. I thought about trying to explain to Josh and Hilary about black holes and María's effect on me. But I chickened out. I was afraid the whole thing would sound too crazy. Of course, Josh already thought I was nuts. I was beginning to believe it myself.

After Josh split off from us, Hilary and I

continued to walk while she chattered on about this new computer game she'd gotten called "Wizard's Island." But when we reached the corner where we part, she stopped talking about the game and looked at me hard. "Listen, Gordon," Hilary said. "If you really like María, make friends with her. Don't pay any attention to Josh."

My cheeks grew warm. "You think I should ignore Josh's warning?"

Hilary rolled her eyes. "Josh pretends to hate all girls except me," she said. "But I wouldn't be surprised if he's just jealous."

"You could be right," I said, remembering how jealous Josh was of me when Hilary and I first became friends. But Josh didn't have to be jealous of María. Even if she and I did become friends, it wouldn't affect my friendship with him and Hilary. Besides, María was only going to be here for three more days. Then she was flying back home to Mexico.

"See you tomorrow," I said as we reached Hilary's street.

Hilary stopped and looked at me strangely. "Don't forget what I said about Josh, okay?" Then she turned and walked away.

6
Mrs. Turnip

For a moment, I stood in the middle of the sidewalk feeling puzzled. Why had Hilary looked at me so strangely and warned me about Josh again? I know Josh can be jealous sometimes. But underneath it all he's one of the nicest — and funniest — guys I know. I don't think he really hates girls, either. He just likes to tease.

I walked on to my house at the end of

Jones Avenue. I only live with my mom, because my parents are divorced and my dad lives in another state.

"Take your shoes off," Mrs. Turnip, our housekeeper, said as I walked in the door. She's very particular about cleanliness. But then, so am I. I slipped off my shoes so I wouldn't track any dirt on the floors or carpets.

Mrs. Turnip's real name is Mrs. Turner. But I think of her as Mrs. Turnip because she's as round as a turnip and, just like the enormous turnip in a story I read, she's hard to budge. Especially when it comes to rules.

I sniffed the air. *Mmm. Chocolate chip cookies.*

Mrs. Turnip opened the oven and took out two trays. She looked at me. "Do your chores, and afterward you can have a couple."

"Okay," I said. "Thanks." Luckily for me, Mrs. Turnip is a great cook.

Mom had left me her usual list of things to do. I fed the two goldfish in the bowl on the coffee table first. Next I emptied the dishwasher, and finally I took out the garbage.

Mrs. Turnip was chopping vegetables at the kitchen counter when I finished my chores. She always makes and eats dinner with me on Tuesday nights because Mom teaches an evening class at City College.

Seeing that I was done with my chores, Mrs. Turnip slid two cookies onto a plate and set the plate on the kitchen table, along with a glass of milk.

"Yum," I said, biting into the first cookie. "These are so-o good."

"Chew with your mouth closed, please," said Mrs. Turnip.

See what I mean about *rules*?

While I was eating the cookies, I thought more about what Hilary had said after Josh left us. *"If you really like María, make friends with her. Don't pay any attention to Josh. . . . I wouldn't be surprised if he's just jealous."*

I almost choked on a piece of cookie. *Caramba!* What if Hilary had been trying to say that Josh was jealous of *me*, not María. Maybe he liked María, too. True, he'd tried to hit her with my ball during dodgeball, but I've seen some guys act like that when they like a girl. Suddenly the puzzle pieces fell into place. The strange look Hilary gave me right before we parted. *"Don't forget what I said about Josh, okay?"* She'd been trying to warn me!

My heart sank. Everybody likes Josh. There was no way María would like *me* better than him. And who could blame her? Es-

pecially after the strange things I'd done in class today.

I shook my head, confused. Maybe I should do something to take my mind off María for a while. "May I help you with dinner?" I asked Mrs. Turnip.

She smiled. "I like a man who offers to help out around the house. How about setting the table?" Opening a drawer, she handed me forks, knives, and spoons.

She'd called me a *man*. I kind of liked that.

"My husband is a big help around the house," Mrs. Turnip said, chopping the end off a carrot. "He works hard all day, same as me, but, unlike some men I know, he doesn't just sit on the couch watching TV when he gets home."

"I don't watch much TV," I said quickly. I wanted her to know I wasn't like those other men, either. "And I always do my chores."

Mrs. Turnip nodded as I set out the silverware. "You'll make a fine husband one day," she said, waving her knife in the air. "There's nothing that attracts a woman more than a hardworking man."

I gulped. I didn't want to get married — not for a l-o-n-n-n-g time, anyway. But if Mrs. Turnip was right, maybe I wouldn't seem like such a loser and María would want to be my friend if she saw how hardworking I was. I just had to think of a way to show her.

7
Showing María

The next morning I got to school early, and this time I didn't just sharpen my pencils and straighten the folders and books inside my desk. I scooped everything out and stacked it on the floor between my desk and María's. Then I grabbed a wet sponge from the sink in our classroom and began washing out the inside of my desk.

I scrubbed extra hard when María came

into the room and sat down. She was wearing white pants and a red T-shirt that matched the heart-shaped red clips in her hair. She watched me for a while. "You must have the cleanest desk in the whole class," she said, finally.

I smiled. "I like hard work. Would you like me to wash yours, too?"

"No, thank you," María said. "Anyway, I'm only here till Friday, remember?"

"Oh, that's right." I frowned. "That's only three more days, counting today."

"I know." Pushing at her glasses, María sighed. "I wish I could stay longer."

"So do I." I blushed. "I mean, I'm sure it must be nice visiting Alicia and her family." Holding onto the dripping sponge, I started back toward the sink. But I'd only gone two steps before I tripped over the books I'd left on the floor. The sponge flew out of my hands and plopped right into María's lap.

"*Caramba!*" she cried, jumping up. The sponge dropped to the floor.

I stared at María. *Good grief!* There was a big gray smudge on her clean white pants. "S-s-sorry," I stammered. Grabbing the sponge, I hurried to the sink with it.

When I came back to my desk, I buried my head in my reading book and wouldn't look at María. I was chicken about what she might say to me if I did. I hoped the gray smudge would wash off of her pants. They looked brand-new.

When it was time to go to the library, I lined up as far away from María as possible. And after we reached the library, I watched to see where she went, then browsed through a shelf at the opposite end of the library.

Hilary walked over to me. "What's going on?" she whispered. "Alicia told me you threw a dirty sponge at María. Why'd you do that?"

I gulped. I hadn't *thrown* the sponge, I'd tripped! María knew that, didn't she? I explained what had happened, and Hilary rolled her eyes. "That is so-o unlike you, Gordon," she said. "You're getting to be as clumsy as Josh."

I hesitated. Should I explain about María and black holes? Then I looked up and saw Josh walking toward us from across the room.

"Did I hear someone say my name?" he asked as he came closer.

"How could you hear that from so far away?" Hilary asked.

Josh wiggled his ears. "Supersonic hearing."

Hilary cocked her head. "Really? Then what'd I say about you?"

Josh grinned. "That you wished you were as smart as me. And that you expect me to go places in life."

Hilary snorted. "Well, you're half-right. I do expect you to go places — and the sooner the better. Like how about now?"

Josh grinned. He and Hilary are always joking around. Now Josh turned to me. "So what's this about you throwing sponges, Gordon?"

Good grief. Is that what everyone thought? I related my sad story again.

After I finished, Josh punched me in the

47

shoulder lightly. "I *told* you girls were trouble," he said. "Especially that Marissa."

"María," I corrected, even though I knew he was teasing.

Hilary glared at Josh. "Girls are NOT trouble!"

Josh held up his hands. "I'm not talking about *you*."

I wondered again if Josh liked María the way *I* liked her. I honestly couldn't tell. But I guess it didn't really matter anymore. If María thought I'd *thrown* that dirty sponge at her, there was no way she'd ever want to be my friend.

Josh left to go check out a book, and Hilary turned to me and said, "How about if I talk to Alicia and explain what really happened? I could even try to find out if María likes you, if you want."

"I guess," I said, trying to pretend I didn't really care one way or the other. But my stomach felt jumpy. I wasn't sure I *wanted* to know what María thought of me. How could she like someone who'd dropped a dirty sponge in her lap — even if it was an accident?

8
Girl Talk

As soon as we got back from the library, it was time for recess. Hilary, Josh, and I stood in line for wall-ball. Josh was first up to play. Hilary tugged on my jacket sleeve. "Alicia's over by the jungle gym," she said, pointing. "I'm going to go talk to her."

I gulped. "Okay."

Biting my bottom lip, I watched her go. In a minute, Hilary reached the jungle gym.

She said something to Alicia, then the two of them moved a few feet away from the jungle gym. They probably didn't want the other girls to hear them talking. Since they were saying stuff about me, I was certainly glad about that!

I looked around for María and spotted her playing jump rope at the far end of the playground with several other girls from our class.

When I glanced back at Hilary and Alicia, they were still talking. I couldn't hear what they were saying, but they sure were waving their arms around a lot. Girls do that, I've noticed. Even my mom does. But I was surprised to see Hilary doing it. She doesn't talk to me and Josh like that. It was like she was speaking a foreign language that only girls know. Then Hilary pointed at me, and Alicia looked over, too.

I ducked my head fast, hoping they hadn't seen me watching them. When I dared to look up again, Hilary was by herself, standing in the same spot she'd been before. I glanced around for Alicia and saw her over by the jump ropers talking to María.

I swallowed hard, wondering what Alicia was saying. After a lot more arm-waving stuff, Alicia ran back to where Hilary was waiting, and María went back to jumping rope.

"Earth to Chicken Boy," said a voice in my ear.

I jumped.

"You're up next," Josh said. He glanced in the direction I'd been looking and frowned. "You've been watching Matilda, haven't you?"

"María," I said automatically.

Just then she looked over at us and waved. I froze, but Josh waved back. Obviously, María didn't have the same effect on him as she did on me.

"Hey," Mark yelled at me. "Are you up or not?"

"I'm up," I said.

Shaking his head, Josh walked to the back of the line as I stepped up to play.

It was lunchtime before I had a chance to talk to Hilary. She and Josh and I were eating lunch at Josh's desk at the back of the room. Thankfully, María was a safe distance away, sitting with Alicia.

Hilary took a bite of her sandwich, then looked at me. "So, I suppose you want to know what I found out."

Josh tore open a bag of chips. "Found out about what?"

"Oh, nothing," I said, wishing Hilary had waited to talk to me alone.

Josh narrowed his eyes. "Are you two hiding something from me?"

Like I said, sometimes Josh gets jealous. "This doesn't have anything to do with you," I said reluctantly. "It's about me and María."

Josh shook his head. "I warned you, Gordon. Girls are trouble."

Hilary reached over and pinched him.

"Ow!" Josh rubbed his arm. "I keep telling you, Hilary. I don't mean *you*!"

"I don't care," said Hilary. "I'm a girl, whether you believe it or not."

I believed it. Especially after watching her do that arm-waving stuff. I unwrapped a bagel. "So what did you and Alicia talk about?" I asked, taking a bite.

Hilary took a sip of milk and swallowed. "First, I explained about the sponge."

"What's to explain?" Josh mumbled with his mouth full of chips.

Hilary ignored him. "Alicia said she'd gotten it wrong about the sponge. María told her it was an accident, too. She said María's not mad at you at all."

That was a relief. "Did she say anything else?" I asked.

Hilary hesitated. Then she glanced over at Josh and grinned.

Josh frowned. "Why're you looking at me like that?"

"Because," said Hilary, "when I told Alicia I knew someone who liked María, Alicia got things all wrong again. She thought I was talking about *you*."

Josh's face turned bright red. "*M-m-me?*" he stuttered.

Hilary laughed. "It *is* funny, isn't it?

Josh unwrapped a sandwich. "So what else did Alicia say?"

"She said María thinks you're nice," Hilary answered.

Josh rolled his eyes, but I thought he seemed pleased. Maybe Josh really *did* want María to like him. After all, he'd waved back at her on the playground while I stood frozen like a stupid statue.

"Did María say anything about me?" I asked quietly.

Hilary shrugged. "Sorry. Recess ended."

At least I knew María wasn't mad at me. If she liked Josh more than me, I could understand. I'd had way too many "accidents." And right then I thought of a way to make sure I wouldn't have any more. When the lunch recess bell rang, I went to talk with Ms. Foster.

9
Moving

Ms. Foster looked up from her computer and studied my face. "Is there a reason you want to move to a new seat?"

I was too embarrassed to explain about María and black holes — so I came up with a different reason. "It's my eyes." I said, squirming because of the lie. "I can see the chalkboard better from the back of the room. Up close it's kind of blurry."

"Maybe you need glasses," Ms. Foster said. She picked up a pencil and tapped it on top of her desk. "Sounds like you may be farsighted. Have you seen an eye doctor?"

I crossed my fingers behind my back. "He said I didn't need glasses. I'm going to see him again after school on Friday, and he's going to fix the problem. Then I can move back to my regular seat on Monday, if that's okay with you."

Ms. Foster raised an eyebrow. "Hmm. Well, I suppose you could sit at that empty desk on the other side of Carl."

Perfect. Like Josh, Carl sat at the back of the room. In fact, Carl would be between me and Josh. "Thanks, Ms. Foster. I appreciate it." I paused. "Could I stay inside for the rest of recess so I can move my stuff?"

Ms. Foster nodded. "That's fine. I was

going to stay in the room to plan lessons, anyway."

After I left her desk, I got a sponge and cleaned the top and the inside of my new desk. Even if it *was* only a temporary move, I didn't want my things to get dirty. I left the sponge on top of my desk as I returned to my old desk to empty it out. Then I carried everything to my new desk and set the stuff on the floor, since the desk wasn't quite dry.

Grabbing the sponge, I stepped around my things and walked over to the sink. As I rinsed out the sponge, I realized I hadn't dropped or tripped over a single thing during the move. Now that I was no longer near María, my behavior had returned to normal.

Back at my new desk, I restacked my books and folders and arranged them neatly inside. Then I rechecked my pencil box for pencils to sharpen. I took three to the side of the room and was sharpening the last one when the end-of-recess bell rang.

Ms. Foster opened the back door, and everyone burst into the room. Josh and Hilary came up to me at the pencil sharpener.

"Hey," said Hilary. "Did you stay in the room all recess?"

I nodded.

"Why?" asked Josh. "Are you sick?"

That's just about the only reason Josh would ever miss a recess. "No, I'm not sick," I said. "I was moving to a new desk."

Hilary frowned. "Why? What was wrong with your old one?"

"Nothing." I moved toward my new desk and they followed me. "I just see better from the back of the room, that's all. But I'm going to move back to the front row on Monday."

"Does that mean you're getting glasses?" asked Josh.

"Not exactly." I sat down at my new desk.

"Contacts?" asked Hilary.

"Um. No." Lying to my friends was even harder than lying to Ms. Foster. I couldn't look at them. I glanced toward the front of the room and my eyes met María's. She stared at me for a second, then turned away.

Josh followed my gaze. "Hmm. María returns to Mexico on Friday." He snapped his fingers. "You moved to get away from her, I bet!"

I didn't say anything. Just shuffled through my desk like I was looking for something. Josh had gotten María's name right this time, I noticed.

Josh grinned. "I'm glad you're finally

following my advice. The only way to avoid girl trouble is to avoid girls."

Hilary held up a fist.

"Correction," Josh said quickly. "Girls that aren't Hilary."

"But why don't you want to sit by María?" Hilary asked after Josh left to get a drink of water. "I thought you liked her."

"I do," I said.

Hilary stared at me, obviously confused.

I sighed. "What do you know about black holes?" I asked.

10
The Truth

As it turned out, my explanation about black holes and María had to wait. Ms. Foster shooed everyone to their seats, and a few minutes later we were off to music class. The rest of the afternoon we were too busy to talk, and we missed afternoon recess again because of an all-school assembly.

"That's TWO afternoon recesses Ms.

Foster owes us," Josh grumbled as we walked back to class afterward.

At the end of the day I grabbed my backpack and jacket, and Hilary, Josh, and I started home together.

"So what do black holes have to do with anything?" Hilary asked as if no time had passed between our earlier conversation and this one.

Josh raised an eyebrow. "Black holes? What're you talking about?"

So of course I had to tell them. "You've noticed that I haven't been myself lately, right?"

"Really?" said Josh. "Then who've you been?"

Hilary rolled her eyes. "You know what he's talking about. Like how he dropped that sponge in María's lap this morning."

Josh kicked a small rock down the side-walk. "And spilled his milk yesterday."

"Eggs-actly," I said. I launched into a description of black holes and the wacky effects they have on other objects. I told them that María was having the same effect on me and that's why I'd been having the weird "accidents." "So I had to move to the back of the room," I concluded finally. I didn't say that I was also sure María thought I was a loser and would rather be friends with Josh than with me.

We stopped walking, because by then we'd reached the corner where Josh splits off from Hilary and me. For a minute, Josh and Hilary stared at me without saying a word. Then Josh scratched his head. "So let me get this straight," he said. "You think María is like a big magnet, and you're *what*? A very large paper clip?"

I sighed. "I guess you could put it that way."

"Aww, man." Josh shook his head. "That's the craziest idea I ever heard."

Hilary looked thoughtful. "Actually," she said, "I think it makes a lot of sense."

"*What*?" said Josh.

"You do?" I said.

"Sure," said Hilary. "Once I asked my mom why she and my dad got married. She said they were attracted to each other and that that's the way love works."

"So?" said Josh. "What's your point?"

"Don't you get it?" said Hilary. "She said they were *attracted* to each other, like black holes attract objects that are near them and magnets attract metal things."

"You're talking crazy," Josh said. "Gordon isn't in love. He *can't* be. It's like I always say, girls . . ."

". . . are trouble," Hilary finished. She tried to sock him, but Josh leaped out of the way.

"Gotta go," he said. "But don't worry, Gordon. Moving to the back of the room was a smart thing to do, and in just two more days your problems will be over." He walked off, whistling.

Hilary watched him leave. She shook her head as we continued to walk. "I don't understand you, Gordon. So you had a couple of accidents. María wasn't mad about the sponge, and I know you like her. How can you make friends with her if you're sitting clear across the room? In two more days she's *leaving*."

I frowned. "Didn't you hear what I told you? About black holes? When I'm near María, weird things happen. I don't know *how* to make friends with her."

Hilary rolled her eyes. "Just talk to her."

I sighed. "I tried."

"Well, maybe you tried too hard," Hilary said.

I wasn't sure what she meant by that, but I didn't ask. We walked on in silence until we got to the street where we part, then we said good-bye.

Josh is right, I thought as I walked the rest of the way home. It was good that I'd moved to the back of the room. There wouldn't be any more "accidents," and in two more days my María problems would be over. But for some reason that thought didn't make me happy.

11
Party Plans

In the middle of math the next morning Carl handed me a note. "It's from Josh," he said.

I held my breath as I opened the note, half-expecting it to be about María. But it wasn't. MS. FOSTER OWES US TWO RECESSES, the note said. DIDN'T SHE SAY SHE'D GIVE US EXTRA RECESS LATER IN THE WEEK? IT'S THURSDAY ALREADY!!

I grinned. SO REMIND HER, I wrote under his message. Then I refolded the note, and passed it back through Carl.

Josh read my note. Then he raised his hand.

Ms. Foster looked up from her desk. "Yes?"

"I was just wondering when we would make up those two recesses we missed," Josh said.

Ms. Foster ran a hand through her tangled, dark hair. "I'm glad you brought that up, Josh. Because, as a matter of fact, it's something I want to talk about. But first I need someone to run an errand for me."

She glanced around the room, and her eyes settled on me. "Gordon," she said. "Could I talk with you for a minute, please?"

Ms. Foster calls on me to run errands a lot, so I didn't think much about it as I went up to her desk. But instead of explaining what she wanted right away, she motioned for me to follow her into the hallway, then closed the door behind us. For a second, I worried that I was in trouble. Maybe she'd seen me passing back Josh's note or had found out I'd lied about my eyes. But that wasn't it at all.

"I want to talk with the class about planning a surprise going-away party for María," Ms. Foster said. "But I need to get María out of the room first."

I saw where this was heading and gulped. "Maybe you could send her on an errand with Alicia?" I suggested.

Ms. Foster shook her head. "I'm asking you because Alicia needs to be in on the planning." She cocked her head. "Besides, you owe me one for changing your seat."

She had me there, of course. But I didn't

give up. "Can't María do the errand by herself?" I pleaded.

"She doesn't know her way around the school. I'm afraid she might get lost going by herself. Besides, I want you to keep her busy for a while." Ms. Foster frowned as if something had just occurred to her. "Is there a reason you don't want to do this?" she asked.

I pulled at the neck of my shirt. "Not really." Talking with my two best friends about my "María problem" was one thing, but I wasn't about to tell Ms. Foster. Not knowing what else to say, I gave in. "All right. What would you like me to do?"

Minutes later, María and I headed to the library. Ms. Foster said she wanted us to look for books on the solar system and check them out for the classroom. We were starting a science unit on astronomy next week. I felt nervous being around María. What if I said or did something stupid again? At the same time, I couldn't help feeling excited. As I said, I love astronomy.

"Did you know that Jupiter has sixteen moons?" I said as we turned the corner and walked down the hall that led to the library. "I've seen some of the larger ones through my telescope."

María's eyes grew wide behind her glasses. "You have a telescope?"

I nodded. "My mom got it for me on my last birthday. It's great. I love looking at planets. And with my telescope, I can see the moon's craters really well."

"This is so amazing," María said. "My birthday is next month, and I've asked my parents for a telescope, too!"

"Really?" My nervousness evaporated. "I didn't know you were interested in astronomy."

"I *love* astronomy," María said. "I have a moon globe at home, and I can find a lot of constellations in the sky. My favorite is the Pleiades."

I nodded. "Oh, yes. The Seven Sisters. Nearly four hundred light years away. You'll be able to see hundreds more stars in that cluster with a telescope."

"I know," María's voice dropped to a whisper as we entered the library. "I can hardly wait. I mean, I've seen pictures on the Internet and in books, of course. But it's not the same as seeing for yourself, right?"

"Right," I whispered.

I gave Ms. Gardner a note from Ms. Foster. Ms. Gardner read it, then smiled. "I guess I don't need to show you where the astronomy books are, do I?" She knows that's my favorite section.

María and I talked the whole time as we piled up stacks of books about the planets, the sun, and the moon. Now that I wasn't nervous anymore, talking to her was as easy as talking to Hilary or Josh. I think I was beginning to understand what Hilary meant when she'd said maybe I'd tried too hard before.

María ran her fingers over the glossy cover of a book on Saturn. "I wish I was staying for another couple of weeks," she said. "I'd like to read all of these."

I wished she was staying, too.

As we carried all the books to the checkout desk, I glanced up at the clock on the wall. Ms. Foster had asked me to keep María away from the classroom for at least fifteen minutes, and we'd been gone for almost that

77

long. By the time our books were checked out, it'd be safe to go back. I was amazed that in the entire time I'd been with María, I hadn't tripped or spilled a single thing! But on the way back to class I nearly dropped the stack of books I was carrying when, right out of the blue, María asked, "Why did you change seats yesterday?"

"It-it was because of my eyes," I stammered. I didn't want to repeat the lie I'd told Ms. Foster, Hilary, and Josh, but what else could I say?

"Oh." María tucked a loose strand of hair behind one ear. She had yellow flower-shaped clips in her hair today. "I was afraid maybe you'd moved because of me."

"Because of you?" I swallowed. "W-why would you think that?"

"Alicia said she'd heard that you liked me. I thought maybe she got the message wrong." María blushed. "Did she?"

I studied the floor. "No," I admitted at last. "She didn't get the message wrong."

"Good," said María. "I'm glad."

She was? I couldn't believe it! I was glad that she was glad — and glad that she had told me. We looked at each other and smiled.

12
Friends

"So what's up with you and María?" Hilary asked as she and Josh and I walked home together that afternoon. "You were out of the room together when we were planning her party, and then I saw you talking with her during the last recess."

I glanced at Josh to see his reaction, but he didn't seem upset. Maybe I'd been wrong about him liking María all along. Liking her as much as *I* did, anyway.

I smiled, remembering how María had laughed at all my chicken jokes during recess, even the really lame ones. "We're friends now," I said simply. "I found out she likes astronomy as much as I do. In fact, she's hoping to get a telescope, too."

Josh groaned. "What good does it do to warn you about girls if you only ignore my warnings?"

Good old Josh. Hilary and I ignored him.

"But what about all the trouble you were having dropping things and tripping and stuff?" Hilary asked as we continued to walk. "Did that just stop?"

I shrugged sheepishly. "I think it was all in my mind." To tell the truth, my ideas about María and black holes seemed pretty silly to me now. Not to mention unscientific. I was glad María would never know.

"I guess I'd better fill you in on the plans for the party tomorrow," Hilary said as we crossed the street.

Josh interrupted. "I don't see how a party makes up for two missed recesses," he grumbled. "I think Ms. Foster is trying to cheat us. The party will be indoors, not outside on the playground where we can play wall-ball."

Hilary and I exchanged a look. "Give it up, Josh," Hilary said. "You'll live."

I grinned. "But if you do eggs-pire, we'll play wall-ball in your honor at your funeral."

"Aww, man," said Josh. "But then I won't get to play with you!"

"That's okay," said Hilary. "You'd just lose anyway."

"So tell me about the party," I said. "Are we bringing presents?"

"Ms. Foster said small gifts would be fine," Hilary said. "I'm going to get María a calendar with pictures from around our state."

"That sounds nice," I said. I knew right away what I wanted to get María, but I kept my idea to myself.

"Ms. Foster said she'll bring a cake," Hilary said.

"I hope it's a white cake," Josh said. "Cake is not the same as recess, but it might help me forgive Ms. Foster."

At school the next morning, it was hard to keep quiet about the party plans. Kids kept whispering and looking over at María. I wondered how she could NOT know that something was going on.

Just before morning recess I asked Ms. Foster if I could move back to my old desk in the front row. "What about your eyes?" she asked. "I thought you were going to see an eye doctor this afternoon."

I shrugged. "As it turns out, I'm seeing very clearly now."

Ms. Foster raised an eyebrow, but she said I could move back.

María stayed in at recess to help me move my stuff back to my old desk. If she wondered why my eyes were suddenly fine, she didn't ask. We talked about a lot of stuff and found out we had other things in common besides liking astronomy. For instance, María is an only child, just like me. And her family has a housekeeper, too. María thought my name for Mrs. Turner was funny.

"He-he-he," she laughed. "Mrs. Turnip." She handed me my pencil box to put away.

"I think I should give our housekeeper a new name, too," she said. "Her real name is Señora Lopez. She's *so* nice."

"What does she look like?" I asked.

"She's very tall and very skinny."

"Like a pencil?" I asked.

María clapped her hands. "That's it!" she said. "You're a genius, Gordon!"

"I am?" I asked.

María nodded. "In Spanish, the word for pencil is *lapiz*. It's perfect! From now on I will call Señora Lopez 'Señora Lapiz.' But only inside my head."

At lunch recess, María wanted to learn to play wall-ball. Hilary, Josh, and I explained the rules and demonstrated how to serve and return the ball. María caught on fast. When she stepped up to play Carl, even Josh was impressed at a couple of the returns she got off. One of them hit the wall at an angle that was impossible to return. "Hey, María's not bad," he whispered.

It was probably as close as he'd ever come to complimenting a girl.

When recess ended, María walked back to class with me and Hilary and Josh. "You all play so well," she said. "Thank you for teaching me. I'm going to keep practicing, and when I get back home, I'll teach my friends to play."

It made me sad to think that just as I was getting to know her, María was going to have to leave and I might never see her again.

13
The Party

When it was almost time for the party, Ms. Foster sent María and Alicia to the office on an errand. It was just an excuse to keep María busy while we set up for the party.

I opened my backpack and pulled out the gift I'd bought for María last night. I put it on top of my desk.

Ms. Foster opened a huge pink box. Inside was a white-frosted cake, decorated with yellow and orange frosting flowers. In the middle of the cake, orange letters spelled out the words "*Adiós,* María." I remembered that *adiós* means good-bye in Spanish. Ms. Foster set the cake on a table at the front of the room.

Nicola and Stephanie tacked a huge banner over the chalkboard. It said WE'LL MISS YOU, MARÍA!

"I think we're ready," Ms. Foster said, placing a stack of napkins on the table beside the cake. She called the office on our room phone. "Please send Alicia and María Garcia back to class now," she said.

"Will do," came the secretary's reply.

When María walked in the door with Alicia, we all yelled "Surprise!"

María's eyes grew wide when she saw the banner and the cake. "For me?" she said. "*Gracias, mis amigos.* You're so nice to me!"

We all knew that *mis amigos* means "my friends."

Ms. Foster cut the cake, then asked Nicola and Josh to pass out pieces to everyone. "Thanks," I said when Josh handed me a piece. "I guess now you have to forgive Ms. Foster."

"Huh?" said Josh.

"The cake," I said. "It's white — just like you wanted."

Josh grinned. "She's forgiven."

I wished I could talk to María while we were having our cake, but she and Alicia were sitting at Stephanie's desk to eat. Afterward, Ms. Foster said we could give María our cards and presents. María sat in a chair at the front of the room, and we gathered around to hand her our gifts. She opened Hilary's calendar first.

"Thank you," said María. "I'll hang it in

my bedroom. Every day it will remind me of my visit."

"Open mine. Open mine next!" kids shouted when María was ready for another gift. I didn't join in the shouting, though. I wanted my gift to be the *last* one María opened.

She got lots of nice presents — like fancy pens and pencils, stationery, and candy. Stephanie and Nicola gave her a fuzzy brown teddy bear. All the girls had to pass it around and hold it. Even Hilary. Josh's gift was a keychain. There was a miniature license plate attached to it — with María's name on it in big letters.

When I was sure she'd opened everything else, I handed my gift to María, crossing my fingers that she'd like it.

María peeled off the shiny red wrapping paper and opened the small box. She smiled when she saw what was inside. "Thank you, Gordon. These are perfect." She held up the decorated hairclips for everyone to see — a shiny silver moon and three gold stars.

Before the bell rang to go home, we cleaned up the room. María disappeared for a few minutes. When she came back, she was wearing my clips in her hair.

Alicia's and María's parents walked into the classroom just as the bell rang. María had told us she'd be going straight to the airport after school in order to be on time for the plane back to Mexico.

I frowned. I'd hoped we'd have more time to talk before María had to leave. "Well, good-bye," I said as she got ready to go.

"Good-bye, Gordon. Thanks again for the clips." She ran to her parents. They started out of the room, then stopped. María said something to her mother in Spanish, and her mother opened her purse and gave María a small card.

To my surprise, María ran back to where I stood. "Here," she said, pressing the card into my hand.

It was blank. "What is it?" I asked.

María turned the card over in my hand so that I could see the writing on the other side. "It's my mother's business card," she explained. She pointed. "Here's my address, and my family's E-mail address, too. We can be pen pals!"

"Eggs-cellent!" I exclaimed, wondering why I hadn't thought of that myself. I tucked the card into my pants pocket.

"Hurry, María!" Alicia yelled from over by the door.

María turned and ran. "*Adiós*, Gordon," she called over her shoulder.

"*Adiós*, María," I called back.

She disappeared through the door with her parents and Alicia.

After María left, I gathered up my things. Then I grabbed my jacket from the coat racks and met Hilary and Josh at the back door.

"Too bad María had to leave," Hilary said as we started to walk home. "I bet you'll really miss her."

I nodded.

"María was okay," Josh said. "For a girl."

Hilary slugged him.

"Ow," said Josh. He grinned. "Like I said, Gordon. Girls are trouble."

I smiled, but I didn't agree. I touched the card in my pocket. Tonight I would send María a message. The first of many, I hoped.

About the Author

Science was never Suzanne Williams's favorite subject in school, but when she was in college she took an astronomy class and *loved* it. She thinks black holes are cool, but friendships are even cooler.

The author of several children's books, including the Children's Choice Award-winning picture book, *Library Lil*, Suzanne lives in Renton, Washington, with her husband, Mark, her daughter, Emily, and her son, Ward. You can visit Suzanne on the web at www.suzanne-williams.com.